There Was a

BOLD LADY

Who Wanted a Star

by Charise Mericle Harper

SCHOLASTIC INC.

New York   Toronto   London   Auckland   Sydney
Mexico City   New Delhi   Hong Kong   Buenos Aires

ISBN 0-439-63241-2

12 11 10 9   9/0

Printed in the U.S.A.   40

First Scholastic printing, November 2003

The illustrations for this book were done in acrylic paint on chipboard, with collage elements.
The text was set in Aunt Mildred, and the display types are Kruede and Hairspray Redhead.

For my mother,

who has always been a very bold lady

There was a bold lady who wanted a star.

I don't know why she wanted a star —
it seemed too far.

There was a bold lady who bought some shoes.

and then stopped for a snooze.

She bought the shoes to catch the star.
I don't know why she wanted a star—
it seemed too far.

SPACE BIRD

EARTH BIRD

There was a bold lady who bought some skates.

She slid and she slipped down hills . . .

and through gates.

She bought the skates
to replace the shoes.
She bought the shoes
to catch the star.

I don't know why she wanted a star—
it seemed too far.

There was a bold lady
who bought a bike.

What's not to like about riding a bike?

She bought the bike
to replace the skates.
She bought the skates
to replace the shoes.
She bought the shoes
to catch the star.
I don't know why
she wanted a star —
it seemed too far.

There was a bold lady
who bought a car.

She drove for a while but she couldn't go far.

She bought the car
to replace the bike.
She bought the bike
to replace the skates.
She bought the skates
to replace the shoes.

She bought the shoes
to catch the star.
I don't know why she wanted a star—
it seemed too far.

There was a bold lady
who bought a plane.

She flew through snow and she flew through rain.

She bought the plane to replace the car.

She bought the car to replace the bike.

She bought the bike to replace the skates.

She bought the skates to replace the shoes.

She bought the shoes to catch the star.

I don't know why she wanted a star—
it seemed too far.

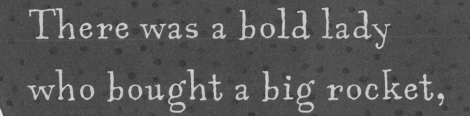

There was a bold lady
who bought a big rocket,

ROCKET SALES

THIS SIDE UP↑

THIS SIDE UP↑

then zoomed up and caught the star in her pocket.

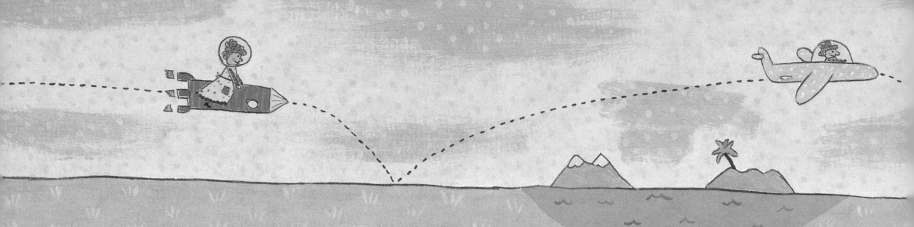

She rode the rocket
back to the plane.

She flew the plane
back to the car.

She skated on skates
back to the shoes.

She drove the car
back to the bike.

She pedaled the bike
back to the skates.

She ran for miles and
didn't stop for a snooze.

There was a bold lady who wanted a star.
Now I know why she wanted the star . . .
to put in a jar. (So it wasn't so far!)